Snapdragon Alley

by Tom Lichtenberg

Copyright 2009 by Tom Lichtenberg
ISBN: 978-0-557-20984-2

Sapphire and Alex

Sapphire was tall for her age, and strong. She was the terror of the fifth grade dodge ball class, but the star of the volleyball team. She was fearless, bold, and constantly in motion. At night she tossed and turned in her sleep and often wound up on the floor along with her blankets. Life for this girl was non-stop adventure, which is why her friend Alex liked to be around her, even if she didn't know when to stop, which could be a problem sometimes. You never knew what it was going to be next, but it was going to be something, that was for sure.

Alex was also ten, and it seemed like they'd known each other forever. They made an odd couple - he was shorter, thinner, and had long shaggy blond hair. From a distance he looked to be the girl and her the boy, with her height and her jet black hair cut short and straight. He was also quieter and by far the more cautious of the two. Alex liked to study things first, puzzle them out, come to an understanding and then mess around. With Sapphire it was jumping in with both feet first and only then considering the consequences.

Together they'd progressed from sandbox to mud puddles, creek walking and ice skating, tree climbing and skate boarding, and every good thing along the way. Now at ten years old they were ready to branch out, see the world, get out there and be life size, even if they weren't quite yet.

"Now's the time", Sapphire declared, and Alex agreed. They'd already decided on code names. She was to be known as Cipher, and he was to be Aleph. It was perfect. Code names first and then disguises and masks. Or maybe not. Cipher was still deciding about that. As for Aleph, he was poring over his collection of official city bus maps, one from each of the past nine years. He had the idea that if you're out to discover the world, a bus map is a decent place to begin.

Spring Hill Lake

Alex took to arranging his bus maps chronologically along his bedroom wall, at a height where he could study them carefully from his upper bunk, and where his little brother Argus could not easily get to them. This led to an endless fascination on the five-year-old's part. He would lie for hours in his lower bunk gazing up at the grids of tiny black lines and bolder red ones as if the secrets of the universe were embedded somewhere in there. Alex knew what all those lines represented, and he was certain they were the key to something more substantial - the way to most efficiently cover the territory.

Alex and Sapphire had different goals in mind for this adventure. Sapphire wanted to go everywhere, or rather, to have been everywhere, on every street. Alex wanted to see everything, to have seen everything, to know what things there were and where. He had a genius for memorization and a desire to fill up his brain cells with tidbits of random knowledge. Sapphire wanted notches on her belt. Her idea was to fan out from where they were, take it one neighborhood at a time, as if it were guerrilla warfare and the surrounding streets were the occupying army. Alex pointed out that this would make their travels that much longer each time. He proposed a more systematic solution; map it out and take the bus. Sapphire had to agree that made a lot more sense.

She had made a list of the streets she'd already been on, and it was a fairly long one. She had relatives in different parts of town, so she could claim substantial portions of those far-flung neighborhoods as conquests. Her list had three columns - the name of the street, a column for her own check marks, and a column for Alex. She figured it counted for both if even only one of them had been there. Alex wasn't so sure about that, but he decided to put off that discussion until later. Alex wanted a strategy. Part of the reason was financial. They would each have to buy a bus pass and that would cost money, so he wanted to make the best use of it.

As he stared at the maps on his wall, he tried to decide how to get it done. Should they cover the farthest regions first, so the job would get easier over time? Should they alternate between remote and distant areas, so they wouldn't get burned out? Should they tackle the safest neighborhoods first, saving the sketchier ones for when they were a little older and more experienced, or should they cross out the bad sections first, just to get them out of the way? He scanned the maps in order from the most recent to the oldest. They were largely the same. Spring Hill Lake was not a huge city, and it hadn't changed much in recent years. Alex didn't even know why he had nine years of bus maps on his wall, only that he liked to skip from one to the next, as if that would freshen his thinking. The bus routes had changed from time to time, it's true, and only the current map was actually useful, but they all gave him ideas. They made him wonder why the 22 no longer went through Skyport , but skirted around it, leaving that neighborhood to the 46 alone. Had demand diminished, and if so, why? Was Skyport not what it used to be?

And how come the 63 went all the way from the southwest to the northeast corner of the city? Was that efficient? That route hadn't changed at all over the nine years he knew about. Was it popular? Would it inconvenience too many people if it were disrupted in any way? He was building up legends about those routes. There once had been someone who could tell him, someone who had known all the answers - his Uncle Charlie, but Charlie wasn't around anymore. He'd been a bus driver, had even driven the 63 once. Alex wished that he could ask him, but all he had now to remember him by were these maps on the wall and some photographs.

The Artist Map

Sapphire's idea was to use highlighter pens to mark up all the streets that she and Alex had "done". Hers would be yellow. His would be blue. That way the ones they did together would be green. Alex smelled a contest and wasn't too big on that idea. Also, he didn't want any of his maps besmirched. He said he would think about it. In the meantime, Sapphire had pestered her dad into bringing home a bus map of her own so that she could get to work in secret, thinking she'd surprise her friend with a fancy presentation. The only problem was she wouldn't know all of his streets so her rendering would be incomplete, but as long as it had all of hers, she'd be happy enough. Her father had just brought home the map the night before, and Sapphire was hiding it in her jacket pocket.

So she sat there fidgeting in the Kirkham boys' bedroom, feeling giddy that she had a secret, and watching Argus watch his brother trace the bus routes with his finger. Sapphire didn't have any brothers or sisters, and had never wanted any, but she did enjoy this little one's company. Argus never said much, and she always wondered why that was. He had the biggest eyes and would sit there on his lower bunk bed half hidden in blankets, just staring and staring at the two bigger kids. Every now and then he'd mutter some word they couldn't understand, and that just made the boy seem even more mysterious to Sapphire. She had concluded that he was actually a cat in human disguise. She figured this was one of the cat's nine lives, that it had chosen to be a boy for life number five, for instance, and that sooner or later, poof! He'd go back to being a cat again.

"We could cover a lot of ground with the old 48", Alex said, showing Sapphire the way on the two year old map. He liked that one the best because of its color scheme, a sort of aqua for the regular routes, and rose for the expresses. Most of the other maps used a more traditional blue and red. This one also had bright green icons for city government buildings and museums, and the index was on the left instead of the right like all the other years. Alex believed that for one year they'd hired an artist to do the map, but he'd turned out to be a some kind of flake, and they'd chucked him at the end of the year and gone back to the same old bureaucrat they'd had before, a guy that Alex imagined to be a slimy looking beanpole by the name of Jimmy Grundling. Grundling was efficient, but had no taste. That's why Alex preferred the "artist map".

Sapphire didn't believe a word of it, and rolled her eyes whenever Alex brought it up, but Argus had absorbed the notion, and kept the idea in his mind that it was better to be an artist than a bureaucrat, even though he wasn't quite sure what either of those were. He just knew it had something to do with choosing colors.

"The 48 covers Westwind, Martinsgate, and Floridan", Alex was saying. "I've never been any of those places except once we went to Martinsgate when my Dad had to stop off at his office, and that was on 11th Street so I've been here, and here", and he traced the side streets where they'd parked and walked.

"How are we going to keep track?" Sapphire wanted to know, steering the conversation back to her master plan. Alex shrugged. Sapphire, who'd been scheming to do the highlight map entirely on her own and present it with a flourish in the future, was incapable of keeping a secret for even one hour, so she jumped up and yelled,

"Surprise!", and whipped her own new bus map out of her jacket and announced,

"We can use this one for the highlighters!!", and without waiting for Alex's response, she hurried over to his desk, where she spread out the map, pulled the highlighters from another pocket and then had to chase them as they rolled off the desk and spilled onto the floor. She fumbled for the blue one, came up triumphant and proceeded to trace the two blocks where Alex had said he'd been.

"It's a start", Sapphire concluded, and she felt that this was the moment when the adventure would finally begin. Alex sighed from his perch on the bunk and just watched as Sapphire found the yellow and started marking all of "her" streets, the ones she could remember at least, mostly around their neighborhood. All the time she did this she was pronouncing their names, followed by "gotcha" or "did ya", or "been there, done that" and laughing with a snort. After she'd performed several of these little acts, she called out to Alex to come down and help. She needed him to do his or at least tell her which ones were his so that she could mark them up. Alex hated to see a bus map being so abused but realized it was no use trying to contain any of Sapphire's enthusiasms at any time, and anyway, at least his own maps were now safe from her predations.

He climbed down, casually mentioned some street names, including a few obscure ones he knew that she'd have trouble finding by herself, so that finally she had to hand him the marker and let him do his own. Between them they had easily covered all of the immediate neighborhoods, and then there were the usual routes to shops and parks and malls. They also identified some downtown spots they knew they'd been to, but weren't sure exactly how they'd gotten there, so they just colored the places themselves. It wasn't long before they'd exhausted their recollections and stood back, a little dismayed at the smallness of their travels in relation to all the little black lines that remained unmarked.

"We haven't been hardly anywhere", Sapphire moaned.

"We'll get there", Alex reassured her. "I mean, that's the plan, right?"

"I didn't know there were so many of them", she sighed.

Alex was thinking that probably most of those streets would not be very interesting, just houses mainly. Maybe it would count if they only turned the corner on those, and didn't have to go down them all the way. He doubted Sapphire would go for that. She would call it cheating, at least at first.

"Did you get your bus pass?" she asked, and Alex nodded. They'd had to work on their parents to let them use their allowance for that. Neither Alex's parents nor Sapphire's dad were happy with the idea, which they'd tried but failed to keep a secret. There were parts of the city that the parents had marked Forbidden, and forced the kids to agree.

"At least until we're older", they'd promised, which to them meant as early as the next day, because, after all, it was true that tomorrow they'd be older than they were today!

"Okay, then", Sapphire said. "Then we're off" and she was gone from the room in a flash, leaving Alex to fold up her map and put the highlighters in his own jacket pocket. Sapphire would never have remembered them until it was far too late.

By the time he got to the front door, she was already on the sidewalk, stamping her feet, and wondering why it was taking him so long. She was, as ever, ready for anything.

The 48 Martinsgate

To get to the 48 they had to walk three blocks, turn left, walk another two, and wait at the stop. There were no published schedules for the buses, not even online. You just had to know, and Alex had a pretty good idea about this one, because he'd been staking it out, doing research. It was a Monday, a holiday so they had no school, and on Holiday Mondays the 48 Martinsgate East ran approximately every twenty minutes after rush hour. Which twenty minutes was any body's guess. Sometimes it arrived around the 0, 20 and 40. Sometimes it was shifted by five or ten minutes either way. Alex had not yet determined a definitive pattern, if there was one.

Fortunately, when they got there, they could see that at least they hadn't just missed one. Several adults were also gathered at the stop, which was a good sign. The grownups were likelier to arrive on time. The ultimate good luck was when one of the adults whipped out a lighter and lit his cigarette. That was almost a guarantee that the bus was just around the corner, and indeed it was. Almost as soon as the guy took his first drag, the huge wheezing silver and green thing pulled around the block and headed towards them. The man muttered a curse and flicked his butt into the road, while Sapphire and Alex cheered and made faces imitating his disappointment.

It made Alex's day just to slide the bus pass through the slot and see the little light go green. He hardly ever got to "do the honors", as he called it when his mother let him. Usually he had to have exact change. Usually he didn't get to ride the bus at all. His mom and dad had no idea it was practically his favorite experience, though you think they might have guessed, from the maps, the posters, the toy buses he collected, his persistent questions about his father's late brother Charles and his employment, but no. Parents were hopelessly clueless, he decided, Sapphire's dad as well. He had the idea that she had some kind of learning disability, all because she hated sitting still.

That was going to be another problem, Alex foresaw. Getting Sapphire to sit still long enough, because buses are slow, and take a long time to get anywhere. Their plan that day was to go as far as Westwind, get off, and walk back, making a sort of maze around the major street, covering two full blocks on either side in a loop back pattern. Westwind was only about a twenty minute ride, while Martinsgate would be at least twice that. He'd have to gauge her persistence and maybe modulate his expectations. He smiled at his thought, at the opportunity to use the word "modulate". Alex loved his words.

Sapphire meanwhile was having no problem sitting still, because the scenery was changing every second. As long as things were new and changing, she could hang on in there, which was one of the reasons she had trouble turning off the television. It was as if they'd calculated her attention span right down to the millisecond - and that would be about right. Her new rule was, never turn the damn thing on. So far she'd gone four days with no TV and was extremely proud of herself.

The bus took off, stopped and started, turned some corners, or barreled down a main drag. She wasn't familiar with the route, and within a few minutes they were in a part of the city she had never seen before. It stunned her to realize that. Here she'd grown up practically a mile away and had never seen that corner grocery store, had never seen the funny bright pink Japanese vegetable stand, had never seen the broken clock on the antique lamp post in front of the now-shuttered hardware store, and she wondered what else she had never seen on that street. Someone might have told her about the life-size plastic horse statue that used to sit in front of that very hardware store, had sat there for more than three generations, had been the pride and joy of the family that had handed down the store from father to son until the realities of modern economics had broken it down for good. She would have loved that horse.

Alex had seen it. It was there until only a couple of years before, and as the bus passed he remembered it and thought of telling Sapphire about it, but he could see that she was glued to the window and wouldn't have appreciated the interruption. He liked to see her like this. She had a half smile that indicated her most benign condition. He would never interrupt a smile like that.

A few minutes later he did have to tap her on the shoulder and tell her they were getting off at the next stop. She turned at him sharply and he thought that maybe she would fight it, but she'd agreed on the plan and simply nodded and pulled the rope to sound the bell. When the bus came squealing to the corner they jumped out of their seats and hopped down the stairs and out the back door.

Snapdragon Alley

Looking to the left and to the right, Sapphire and Alex couldn't make up their minds for a few minutes. There seemed to be no difference to the side streets - each one contained an array of single family homes with picket fences enclosing small front yards. None of them looked like adventure. Alex sighed, thinking maybe just peering down the way would count, and hoping his friend would go along with that, but his expectations were realistically low. She was not going to be deterred and was not ready, yet, to modify the rules.

"How about this one?" she proclaimed, gesturing at a street sign reading 'Poindexter'.

"Might as well", Alex agreed, and down the street they went. No one was on the sidewalks, though you might have expected to see some children playing outdoors. Inside a few of the homes they could see the televisions flickering, but every house was pretty much like the last. Some were pale blue, some beige, an occasional pink or yellow. Some had tiny porches. Most did not. There were about twenty houses to the block, and Alex and Sapphire dutifully wound their way around several of them, from Poindexter to Carter to Haymaker and Sansome, round and round through Glenwood Court and Glenwood Place, making sure to circle around the cul-de-sacs, until finally making their way back to Martinsgate Avenue, a few blocks from where the bus had dropped them off.

Sapphire looked at Alex. Alex looked at Sapphire.

"This is not an adventure", she said, and he sadly nodded in agreement.

"In fact", she continued, "this sucks."

"Yup", said Alex.

"Change of plans?" she asked.

"Got to", Alex admitted. He'd kind of known this wasn't going to work.

"Donuts?" she continued, and since they were standing right in from of Millie's Donuts, they agreed to go in and snag a few while they thought the matter over.

Alex liked the plain old-fashioned. Sapphire, anything with jelly inside. It was typical, Alex thought, as he watched the purple goo spread down her chin. If it's messy enough, she can't resist!

He had pulled the map out of his pocket and was using the blue and yellow highlighters together to mark down the half a dozen streets they'd bored through. It barely added a spot to the overall situation.

"There is no way", Sapphire said, with her face full of crumbs, "that I am going to march down all those stupid streets with nothing and nobody on them. I don't care. What's the point?"

"Because they're there?" Alex suggested.

"I wish they weren't", she pronounced. "New rule. It has to have something on it, okay? Only streets with something on them."

"Something being anything but houses?"

"Or apartments".

"Like a business?"

"Any business at all."

"Even if it's just a psychic?"

"Especially if it's a psychic", Sapphire laughed. "Those we gotta do. If there's a psychic, we're going in, okay?"

"But how do we know for sure?"

"We can just look down 'em. We can be pretty sure, I think. No more dead-ends. No more 'courts' or 'places'. No more streets that curve around a little going nowhere. Let's use a different color to mark them out of bounds."

"Red?"

"Good idea. I'll bet we could just 'red out' a whole bunch of the city right now, just by looking at the squiggly lines".

Alex looked it over and was pretty sure he agreed.

"We can still cover all the neighborhoods", he said, "just not every house".

"And we have to go into every kind of business at least once, okay?"

"Even liquor stores? They'll throw us out."

"Let 'em. We just have to go into one of them one time, and we'll make a list. We'll write down every kind of store we go into and how many times, but we only have to do each kind one time, okay?"

"Okay", Alex nodded. He knew that when it came to rewriting all the rules, there was never any holding her back. She could always come up with more new rules per second than anyone.

"Write down donuts", she ordered, as Alex pulled out the little blue notebook he always carried around.

"We might need index cards", he muttered, as always preparing to organize.

"We could do a whole bunch right now", Sapphire's eyes shone, as she looked out across the street at a whole row of little shops - "shoe repair, pizza, water ... what?" she guffawed, "there's a water store over there across the street. Oh man, we gotta go in there. We'll set a record for the most different kind of stupid", and then she was already out the door heading for the corner before Alex even knew that she'd stood up.

The chase was on. Sapphire was determined to walk in and out of every business on the street, first on one side and then the other, and Alex did his best to keep up and keep notes too. Somehow she'd managed to shift the priorities again. They had started out doing streets, and now they were doing businesses. He never knew how she managed to switch contexts every time, and once she got started, there was no stopping her until she ran out of space or time or both. Fortunately for their feet, she was still following the original plan to head back the way they'd come on the bus, so it was just a matter of walking in and out of every shop on Martinsgate Avenue for the entire two miles. Alex was dutiful, but dragging by the end of it.

Later, when he was glad to be home and resting on his bunk bed, he looked over his wall of maps again. He still had dreams of achieving his original plan, but with Sapphire it might not be possible. He couldn't even keep her on the same track for even a whole day.

"I should have known better", he said to himself. "It was never going to happen".

His eyes followed once again the line of the 63 Venezia, how it cut across the city in a diagonal zigzag from the southwest to the northeast, how it stayed the same from year to year to year, when all the other routes seemed to get adjusted and re-arranged. He decided he would take that bus, alone if he had to, all the way from end to the other and back.

While he was dreaming of the 63, he didn't see his little brother come into the room and climb halfway up the bunk bed ladder. He didn't notice until Argus suddenly announced,

"How come that one street disappeared?"

Alex sat up and looked at where his brother was pointing on the artist map - way up in the farthest northeast corner of the city, where the 63 Venezia came to an end, and Alex saw it, and saw it for the first time, although he must have looked at that map for a million hours, that the 63 had indeed changed, once, and only once, during that one year of the artist map. It went one block further than it ever did before or after. That one block was a very small street which seemed to come to a sudden end just shy of the city line, and the map had the street's name spelled out in the tiniest of print. Alex had to grab a magnifying glass and press his face up against the wall to make out the words, 'Snapdragon Alley'.

He looked down at Argus, who was still perched halfway up the ladder.

"I don't know", Alex said. "But I'm sure going to find out".

The 63 Venezia

The following Saturday, Alex took off bright and early, before anyone else was awake, before anyone else could ask him what he was up to. He didn't want to have to make any explanations or get anyone's permission. All week long he'd been thinking about the 63 Venezia. He knew he'd have to take the 46 Hopland first to get to the beginning of the line, and the 46 did not run very often, especially on weekends. It was about a ten block walk just to get to the 46 stop, and he was there by seven fifteen. Seven fifteen on a Saturday, he reminded himself. He didn't think he'd ever even been awake that early before on a Saturday, except maybe on a Christmas once.

It was chilly and he'd forgotten to bring a warm enough jacket, so he stood there on the sidewalk shivering, and thinking about the mission. His mission, not Sapphire's latest, which had rapidly evolved from visiting one of every kind of store to visiting each and every store to visiting only weird and stupid stores to leaving cryptic notes in stupid stores, alerting people to their own stupidity for even being there. This latest plan led Sapphire on an all-night cryptic note writing binge, in which she became The Masked Revealer. In this guise she penned small colored index cards with messages such as "Ever wonder where your life went?igned The Cipher", and "It's not too late to do something better with your day, signed The Cipher". These she planned to randomly distribute in gifty boutiques, wine shops, the hat shop she couldn't believe even existed (who the heck wears hats? she'd blurted out to the dismay of the shopkeeper), and the place that sold only heart-shaped objects. They had discovered these delights on the day they took the 16 Visola to the upscale Mizzerine district.

That was all a lot of fun, but exhausting, and Alex was all Sapphired-out, as he liked to put it. She wasn't interested in his 'quest for the end of the line', as she put it. At least she wasn't interested yet. With Sapphire, everything was only a matter of time and mood.

Argus had wanted to come with him, had begged him even, and Alex had promised to consider it, but knew there was no way he would be able to talk his parents into it. They barely let him take Argus to the playground down the street! Mister and Mrs. Kirkham were certainly well-meaning, but as fearful and paranoid as any parent of their time, and since they were hardly ever around to do stuff with the kids, the kids ended up not going anywhere, mostly. This had led Alex to become so restless that he couldn't bear it anymore. It began with the bus maps, but they were only the expression of his yearning. As soon as he became old enough, and he'd hammered out a deal that the magic number was ten, he was going to go places, and so he did. He just hadn't worked his little brother into the deal yet.

So he was alone on Saturday morning when he took the 46 to the southwest corner of the city, and waited there at 39th and Pine for the 63 Venezia. He didn't have to wait there very long. When it came, he flashed his pass and took the seat right behind the driver, a dark-haired, blue-capped man who could have been thirty or fifty. Alex couldn't tell. He'd said good morning but the driver had only grunted.

"I tried to get him to talk", Alex said to Argus later that day, when the two of them were alone in the kitchen eating cookies and drinking root beer. "But he wasn't one to talk. That's exactly what he told me. Look kid, I'm not one to talk". Alex laughed at his own imitation of the gruff and surly driver.

"I told him our Uncle Charlie used to drive this route. I told him, but he said he never heard of any Charlie Kirkham or any other Kirkham as a matter of fact."

"Did you ask him about the street?" Argus wanted to know.

"Yeah, I did." Alex said, "I didn't know how to bring it up at first, without sounding goofy, you know. So I said my Uncle Charlie told me that the route had only changed once in all the years since the very first 63, and you know what he said?"

"Uh-uh", Argus mumbled through a mouthful of chocolate.

"He said it ain't never changed, boy, not even once. Long as the 63 has been around it's been the same damn thing, day in and day out, month after month and year after year. They tell me, he said, they tell me it's the only route of its kind, like it's some kind of treasure. You should hear the old-timers talk, he said. Every other route, they tinker with, they tell me, but the 63, don't nobody got the balls to touch that thing".

At this both Alex and Argus started giggling and snorting root beer all over the table.

"He really said balls?" Argus choked.

"Don't nobody got the balls, that's what he said. I asked him why was that and he said something about how the route was some kind of sacred cow. I don't know what that means. Politics, he said. It was all about the powers that be. I didn't know what he was talking about but I told him that Uncle Charlie said it changed one time - I was lying of course. Uncle Charlie never told us that. We just saw it on the map, right? I told him he said it used to go another block at the other end." The driver just laughed at me, and said

"I don't know no Uncle Charlie", the driver told me, "but you just sit back and see for yourself. This bus is going to go as far as it can. There ain't no 'nother block. You'll see"

"After that he wouldn't talk to me anymore, and people started getting on the bus, pretty soon it was filling up so I sat back and watched the road. The 63 goes a long way, Argus, all the way through the city. I've never seen so much of Spring Hill Lake before. It goes through nice parts, really nice parts, and bad parts, really bad parts, then you're downtown and then you're out again, and through some more bad parts, some not so bad, and then you're at the end. The driver made an announcement about it so I got off."

"And what did you see?" asked Argus, who was all attention now.

"Nothing", Alex said. "It was like the driver told me. There is no other block. At the end of the line there's a vacant lot, a big one, like there used to be something there but way way long ago, because it's nothing but a field of weeds and broken cement. I poked around for a bit but there was nothing to see. On one side there's a row of old houses, all of them looking like they used to be painted red, once upon a time, with white stairway railings coming down along stone steps, all chipped and worn. On the other side there's nothing but what used to be a factory or a warehouse, but it's now just a wall of graffiti and broken glass,"

Argus sat quietly, thinking, as Alex paused to take a long, slow drink. He was forming the picture in his mind, seeing everything his brother was describing to him, and he seemed to almost be there. He looked to Alex like he often did, in a trance, in another place and time. Alex used to wonder if his brother was retarded - until the little bugger suddenly started reading chapter books one day when he was only three. Then he wondered if he was a genius! By now he'd gotten used to it. Argus was "unusual". That's how Alex would describe him to his friends, with pride.

"I want to go", said Argus.

"It's like I told you", Alex replied. "There's nothing there. I waited for the next 63 bus back. This time the driver was a lady and she right away told me not to bother her. No talking to the driver. So I didn't even get to ask if she knew Uncle Charlie, and I think she might have, because it looked like she'd been driving for a long time, not like the first driver, who told me he'd been on the wheels for eighteen months, three weeks and two days, as if he was counting up to some magic number when it would all be over."

"Eighteen months isn't long enough", Argus said. "He wouldn't have known about the route".

"He said the old-timers told him".

"They were lying to him", Argus declared. "They don't want anyone to know."

"Know what?" Alex asked.

"About the route", Argus said, "about why it changed, and why it changed back"

Alex just shook his head. Let the kid play make-believe, he thought. The reality is, he told himself, the reality is that reality is.

The 46 Hopland

The next time Sapphire came over, Alex was determined not to tell her anything about his little trip, but she was the one who pulled out the marked-out map and noticed the blue line extending all the way across the city along the 63 bus line.

"When did you do that?" she asked.

"Last weekend", Alex had to admit. Sapphire absorbed the information quietly, calculating in her mind exactly when that had been possible, including the fact that he had gone without her. She didn't ask him why, but just grunted a little and asked him if he'd seen anything interesting.

"Some of the neighborhoods looked okay", he volunteered, trying to decide whether he should pretend he'd really just been scouting the line for points of interest.

"He went to Snapdragon Alley!" Argus suddenly piped up from beneath his blankets. Sapphire was startled for a moment. As usual, she hadn't even known the little guy was in the room. He had almost perfected his invisibility routine.

"Where's that?" Sapphire inquired.

"It's the street that disappeared", Argus said again. Sapphire looked up at Alex.

"What is he talking about?" she asked. Alex shrugged. He didn't want to talk about it, but Argus wouldn't let it go.

"It's only on the artist map", the little boy announced, leaping out from under the covers and climbing halfway up the ladder. He stretched out as far as he could and pointed. Sapphire got up from the desk chair and came over. She was tall enough to see the top of the maps easily.

"Where?" she couldn't tell what Argus was pointing at.

"I'll show you", Alex said, and leaned over his bed and tapped the map at the very end of the 63 Venezia.

"Now it's here", he said, "and now it isn't", pointing at the next map on the wall. "And it wasn't on any other maps before either. But it's just a vacant lot. Must have been a misprint or something."

"A misprint with a name on it?"

Sapphire was dubious. She could barely make out the tiny font, but she was shaking her head.

"A vacant lot? That doesn't sound right."

"It was two years ago", Alex said. "Maybe they had some plan to make it a real street, so they put it on the map, but then the plan fell through."

"That makes more sense", Sapphire agreed. "I could check with my dad". Her father was on the city's planning board. He knew about all sorts of projects that never happened.

Sapphire being Sapphire, she was out of the room and down the hall before anyone knew it, on the phone, calling her dad. It didn't occur to her that he might be in a meeting, that he might be busy, that he might not be available. She was determined and was going to do whatever it took. Her father's assistant didn't even bother trying to put her off. She'd come to know the futility of that, so she just patched the girl straight through, and her father had no choice but to answer her questions, keeping his business partners waiting there in his office, tapping their feet.

A few minutes later she was back, triumphant.

"Check it out!" she proclaimed. "There was never any such thing as Snapdragon Alley. My father says that vacant lot used to be an apartment building, a crummy project that was torn down a long time ago because of health concerns, and there's never been anything done with the property since. No plans, no nothing. He says the owner of the lot refuses to sell at any price. Nobody even knows the guy, he just has a mailbox and every time someone asks him about it he sends a postcard in reply with one word on it - NEVER. My dad says it's something of a legend around City Hall, but he never heard the term Snapdragon Alley. I told him about the bus map and he said it must have just been some kind of mistake."

"I guess so", Alex said, disappointed. He was hoping his idea that there was had been a plan was going to turn out right.

"I want to go anyway", Argus said.

"Yeah", Sapphire agreed, "We've got to."

"There's nothing there", Alex protested.

"I don't care", Sapphire replied. "We're going."

And that was that. Alex tried to say that his parents would never let him take Argus all the way across town, but Sapphire assured him that if they lied and said they were taking him to the playground, no one would ever know the difference, and that's how Alex found himself saying what Sapphire told him to say and doing what Sapphire told him to do, pretty much like any other day, and before he knew it the three of them had collected whatever spare change they could find around Alex's room and headed out the door ("just going to the playground, Mom!") and were on the 46 Hopland, and on their way

The Old Geez

Sapphire liked a lot of the neighborhoods they passed through on their way across town, and asked Alex to remember the place with the old soda fountain, and the barber shop with the Christmas tree in the window all year long, and the tanning salon she thought was a hoot, and any number of other shops and streets that kept Alex busy making notes in his notebook. In the meantime, Argus was just in heaven, his face pressed up against the window, his eyes radiating pure joy. Even his ears were humming with the beautiful sounds of the bus wheels grinding, and the back doors creaking open, and the squealing of the brakes as they came to many halts. The trip could not have been too long, as far as he was concerned, but finally they did arrive at the end of the line, and the three kids tumbled out onto the dirty sidewalk at the corner of Visitation and Cogswell.

They watched as the bus made its turnaround and rode off back down Visitation. Everything was just as Alex had described; the long row of decrepit red row houses, the abandoned factory, and in between, the vacant lot where they thought Snapdragon Alley should have been. Argus led the way into the lot, picking his way around outcroppings of former foundation. Far off at the other end of the lot, they could see the bent figure of an old man carrying something like a vacuum cleaner around the lot. Sapphire pointed him out.

"Uh-oh", she said, "something crazy on aisle seven", and the other kids laughed. She kicked a few rocks and stuck her hands in her pockets. She looked at Alex, who didn't have to say 'told you' for her to know exactly what he was thinking. Argus was thoroughly enjoying himself, as he leaped from one spot to another, bending down, peering into crannies and under stones, pushing aside weeds, and generally acting like he was looking for something in particular.

"Find anything?" Alex called out.

"I think so", Argus declared, and he ran back holding up something green and shiny in his hand. It looked like an ornament, a tiny stained-glass dragonfly.

"Keep it for me?" Argus asked his brother, and ran back off. Alex put the little treasure in his pocket. He knew about Argus and his collections. Such things were terribly important to his brother.

Sapphire nudged him, and gestured toward the old man, who was now approaching them as rapidly as he could with his age and that heavy bit of equipment he was carrying. Alex could now see it was a metal detector.

"Hey, you kids", the old geezer shouted.

"Uh-oh", Sapphire said again. "Looks like trouble now."

The old man repeated that phrase every few steps until he finally got up close to them. Sapphire had thought he'd be one of those smelly homeless guys but it turned out he was a clean old man, dressed way out of date but neatly, clean-shaven. He didn't have a mean face but he was scowling.

"What are you kids doing here?" he asked. "This is private property".

"Nothing, sir", Alex volunteered.

"Are you looking for something?", Sapphire asked, as pleasantly as she could. "Maybe we could help you find it"

"No!" the old man shouted. "and no", he continued, answering the second question. He looked down around the ground where they were all standing, and shook his head.

"I'm never going to find it", he muttered. "Been looking for months."

"What is it?" Sapphire asked, but the old man just shook his head and didn't answer. Alex drew out the tiny glass artifact from his pocket and held it out to the man, reluctantly. He was hoping it wouldn't get snatched away, but the old man, after glancing at it, shook his head again.

"Nope. Not it", he murmured, "But thanks. Thank you for asking". He almost smiled, though he was trying as hard as he could not to.

Argus came running up, shouting.

"Alex! Sapphire! You're not going to believe it", and when he got up close to them he stopped and held out his hand. Resting in his palm was a small, thin copper ring.

"A washer?" Alex asked.

"Good find", Sapphire said sarcastically, but the old man dropped his machine and stepped over to the little boy and nearly yelled,

"Let me see that!".

Argus took a step backward, but composed himself and kept his hand out steadily and let the old man bend over it and examine the ring.

"May I?" asked the old man gingerly, and Argus nodded. He took the ring from the boy and held it up to the sky. It sparkled as he turned in a circle, and then, holding the ring with his thumb and index finger on the top and bottom, he seemed to be aiming it at a spot on the abandoned factory wall.

"It's no use", he said, after a few moments. "If only Charlie was here. Charlie would know what to do."

"Charlie?" Alex gasped.

"Charlie Kirkham", the old man said. "That guy knew all about the magic stuff".

Mason Henry

"Charlie Kirkham was my uncle, our uncle!" Alex cried out.

"Yeah", said Argus, although he could barely remember Uncle Charlie, who'd vanished into thin air two years before and was since presumed dead. Alex alone was certain that Charlie was still alive, though of course he could never explain why he had this feeling, or where Charlie might have gone or why. He had all sorts of theories about the mystery - a secret life, a hidden treasure, a criminal flight - but nothing that really fit with the actual man, who was a fairly simple, regular guy; a bus driver, a bowler, a handyman, a casual sports gambler, a boy who never quite grew up into his six foot two, two hundred twenty pound body.

Charlie's older brother Robert, Alex and Argus' father, had a long list of disapprovals when it came to his younger sibling. Charlie was never smart enough, or bold enough, or disciplined, strong-willed, or ambitious enough - the traits that Robert had in over-abundance and the only ones he valued. Alex used to chuckle when his dad complained that Charlie didn't have any drive - after all, he drove a bus all day! What more could his father want?

Alex's mother, Mary, was sure that Charlie had gotten in trouble with his gambling, had met up with some "bad characters" who had "made an end of him". She had watched way too many crime shows on TV. She tried not to mention the man, "so as not to upset the children", but when she did it was with a sigh and to expect his corpse to come floating down the Wetford River any day.

But Alex believed his Uncle Charlie when he told him he never gambled serious money, because he never had any, just a few lousy bucks here and there on the Sea Dragons football team. There was another side of Charlie that maybe only Alex had ever seen, and only rarely, when during a long lazy game of catch, Charlie would start chattering about things he'd seen that no one knew about, things he couldn't talk about, things that nobody would believe.

"I'd believe you", Alex reassured him, and Charlie smiled and nodded.

"I believe you'd believe me", he laughed.

"So tell me", Alex pleaded.

"Another time", said Charlie, and so it happened the same way the few times the subject came up, but that promised other time never came. One morning Charlie Kirkham boarded his bus for the last time. He drove to the end of the line, walked off the bus, and was never seen again.

"My Uncle Charlie disappeared", Alex told the old man, "do you know where he is?"

"I wish I did", the old man replied. "I really wish I did". He shook his head sadly.

"The last time I saw your Uncle", he continued, "was right about where we're standing now".

"But I'm forgetting my manners", he said. "Here I am talking with the nephews and niece of Charlie Kirkham and we haven't even been properly introduced"

"Actually", Sapphire spoke up, "I'm no relation, just a friend. Sapphire."

"Sapphire!" the old man said, "what an extraordinary name, and what a perfect fit! Indeed. Mason Henry, that's me", and he held out his hand and shook Sapphire's.

"Alex Kirkham, and my brother Argus", said Alex.

"I'm Argus", said the little one, pointlessly.

"Very pleased and honored to meet you both", said Mason Henry, shaking their hands in turn.

"What were you trying to do with that ring?" Sapphire asked, "and what did you mean about magic?"

Aha", said Mister Henry, "right to the point. Yes, of course. That must have seemed awfully strange. You probably think I'm off my rocker", he chuckled. "But just you wait. Just wait. When you hear the rest, you'll really think I am! But why are we standing out here in this empty lot. Come along, my house is just over there, at the edge of the field, the last house in the row. Would you like some milk? I probably don't have any. But I have soda. Do you like soda? What do kids drink anyway? I have no idea. I haven't talked to an actual child in years!"

They followed Henry to his house, one of the worn-down structures that lined the left side of what must have been Snapdragon Alley, although the sign on that narrow street read Trent Blvd.

"Hardly a boulevard", Sapphire commented as they crossed it. The street was barely more than a ditch.

"True enough", said Mason Henry, "but then again I once saw a dirt road curving through the middle of a vast sugar beet field that was called John F. Kennedy Boulevard. We're at least a little more modest here."

The inside of the house was as dilapidated as the outside, containing two old dusty and overstuffed chairs in the front room with their stuffing leaking out, and a rickety aluminum table in the kitchen, with two folding chairs beside it.

"Sorry there's no good place to sit", the old man said, rummaging through the fridge for a few cans of Coke.

"It's okay", said Alex, who was really kind of shocked at the dirt and disorder all around. This was decay of a kind he had never experienced before.

"It's just me here now", Mason Henry continued. "Henrietta's been gone about two years now."

Sapphire and Alex exchanged glances, warning each other not to laugh at the idea of a Henrietta Henry. Brief nods assured each other they wouldn't.

"That's too bad", said Argus. "I'll bet you miss her".

Once Again Alex was struck by the fact that his little brother, barely out of diapers as far as he was concerned, always seemed to say exactly the right thing at the right time.

Alex and Sapphire picked up the folding chairs and everyone moved into the front room, where they sat in a half-circle around the big picture window that overlooked the vacant lot. Mason Henry gestured out the window.

"It's all still there", he said mysteriously. "I believe it. Can't see it, but I believe it."

"What's all still there?" Sapphire asked.

"Snapdragon Alley", Mason Henry replied. Alex nearly choked on his drink. He was certain that none of them had mentioned that name until now.

The Spot

"I don't understand", said Alex. "There was a Snapdragon Alley on the bus map two years ago. Before then it was never there, and since then it's never been either."

"It was on a map?" Mason Henry seemed genuinely surprised. "That might be the strangest thing of all. On a map?"

"Well, why wouldn't it be?" Sapphire wanted to know, "if it was a street and it was there, then why shouldn't it be on a map?"

"Well, considering it's not really a street", Mason Henry murmured, "and the little fact that it's not strictly what you might call 'there' ..." his voice trailed off.

"Now I'm even more confused", said Alex. "Either something is or it isn't. Either it's there or it's not."

"How to explain", Henry began, "how indeed to explain." He rubbed his chin and started out the window again.

"It's yours!" Argus suddenly spoke up. "That land out there is yours."

"Yes, it is", said Mason Henry. "It really belonged to Henrietta, but I suppose it's all mine now"

"You're the one who won't sell", Sapphire put it. "My father works for the city and he told me about it."

"Never!" flashed the old man angrily. "I'll never sell and I'll make sure they never get their grubby paws on it too. If only I could make sure, that is." He paused, and then quietly said, "One thing happeneth to them all ..."

"But why?" Alex asked

"Because of Snapdragon Alley", Argus quietly told him.

"Did you ever hear of The Spot?" Mason Henry looked at all three of the children in turn.

"Depends", Sapphire replied. "Is it a nightclub?"

"No, no, no", Mason Henry said, "it's a place, a magical place, you might say, in this world but not only in this world, in other worlds as well, and at the same time. It's a crossroads, a junction, an intersection where realities meet"

"Like parallel universes?" Alex had read his share of science fiction.

"Not quite", said Mason Henry. "There is only one universe."

"Other dimensions?" Sapphire asked. She had read exactly the same books as Alex.

"Facets, you might say", the old man shrugged. "More like facets. When you think dimensions you think direction and shape. It's not quite that. It's a vantage point, a view. If you look the right way, at the right time, you can see it, all of it, very clearly and very much right there", and again he pointed out the window.

"So the ring", Argus said softly, and then more loudly he added, "can you tell us what it looks like?"

"In a way, my dear boy", beamed Mason Henry, and he gave Alex a look signaling his great impression of the little one.

"The way Henrietta saw it, you would think it's nothing special, not really. Just a little housing development. Cute little houses, with lawns and picket fences. Maybe a dozen or so. A little park in the middle with a playground for the children. The road itself is more of a path - Snapdragon Alley, that is. No cars on it. No parking. Odd thing, that."

Mason Henry was silent for a moment.

"But then again", he continued, "the way Charlie saw it was nothing like that at all. He said it was like a big open warehouse, all windows all around and no doors you could see, just all green glass and filled with plants and creatures he could not describe."

"Were there any people in there?" Alex asked. He was thinking, how can anybody live in a place that isn't even there, or at least isn't visible. Are the people invisible too? Did they all just vanish like Uncle Charlie? Is he one of them? Is he still there?

"Hard to say", said Mason Henry, and he shook his head. "I can't even say one thing that's for certain about that place".

"Sounds like my house", Sapphire said.

Everyone laughed, but the room was full of tension now. Alex was not the only one harboring a million questions.

"I know what you're thinking", Mason Henry said. "To tell you the truth, I haven't ever even seen the place myself. I just know what Henrietta and Charlie told me. I've been looking, I can tell you that. Well, you saw me, out there scavenging around. I'm certain there's a way to do it. Charlie could. Henrietta could."

"You said something about magic", Sapphire reminded him, and the old man shook his head.

"Is it magic or is it only some kind of advanced science?" he asked the air in general. "There's a famous saying about that, I think"

"The only thing I know for sure", he continued, "is that there is a way. I used to see Henrietta carrying around certain objects. I would ask her about it and she'd tell me it was none of my business. Kept me in the dark, I don't know why. There are things you're better off not knowing, she'd say. It can't do you any good, and what you don't know can't hurt you. But some times, she'd get so excited she couldn't help herself. She'd yell for me. Mason, come here. Come quick. Snapdragon Alley is back again! But I could never see it."

"It comes and goes", Argus muttered, "but how did she know?"

"She was looking all the time", Henry told him. "She never figured it out completely. One day she'd be carrying around a blank book, another day it was a compass, then again a watch, or a globe, or an hourglass. I've kept all those items", Henry said, and pointed to a cabinet by the wall, where on shelves behind glass doors those very items sat.

"I take them out like she used to do, and I carry them around like she used to, and I come home and I put them back on the shelf"

"Like she used to", Argus finished the sentence.

"Exactly", agreed Mason Henry.

"And Uncle Charlie?" Alex wanted to know. "How did he find the place?"

"Oh, Charlie seemed to know all about it", said Mason. "From the very first day he showed up here, driving that 63 Venezia. He'd get off the bus and take a stroll around the edges of the lot. He had a ring that he'd hold up to his eye, just like I did today. He'd hold it up and move his head around, then stop, and walk straight in that direction. He'd go right across the lot. Then he'd head back to the bus and turn it around for the return trip. Some days he came as a passenger, not the driver.

And sometimes when he'd walk across that lot he'd simply vanish. I saw it happen once myself. That's how we first found out about it, Henrietta and me. Up until then it was just an empty lot to us, like it is to everybody else."

"It was Henrietta got to talking to Charlie, got him to tell her what it was, and then he showed it to her. He told her some, but far from everything about it, and she told me even less."

"It's too bad", Alex said, but secretly he was thrilled. More than ever he was convinced that Uncle Charlie was still alive. He felt he knew for a fact now that Charlie was merely in some other dimension, or facet as the old man called it, and that all they had to do was figure out the secret and they could go there too and find him.

It might be easier said than done, he admitted. Considering they had no idea whatsoever.

On the way back home on the very same bus that Charlie Kirkham used to drive, Sapphire voiced the thought that worried each of them.

"The old man might be crazy", she said.

"That's possible", agreed Alex.

"Likely, even", Sapphire added. "If we told anyone what he told us today, that's the first thing they would say."

"And then they'd say we should never go back there ever again", said Alex. "I know that's what my parents would say. My mom never even wants to hear Uncle Charlie's name, and my dad would say it's just like Charlie to wander off into some unproductive and unlucrative dimension". He laughed.

"That's why we can't tell anyone", said Argus

"Agreed", Sapphire said.

"Heck, we can't even tell anyone anything about today", said Alex. "Remember, we told mom we were just taking you to the playground."

"I need to think", the little boy said, and he turned his head toward the window and stared at the passing shops and streets.

When they finally arrived home, they found their mother hadn't even noticed they'd been gone. Back in their room, the boys collapsed on their beds, exhausted, but neither one could help but look at the artist map, and at that point at the end of the 63 line.

Kindergarten

The mystery was interrupted by school. The fifth-graders were suddenly swamped with homework and exams, and even Argus felt that kindergarten was an unwelcome burden. It was the first time he'd ever resented it. While his friends Max and Molly and Ayesha were happy to be back skipping around on the blacktop, Argus' mind was far from tag and jump-rope. He had caught the fever, and instinctively he knew it, knew that what he was feeling now was the same thing that had once caught hold of his Uncle Charlie and never let go. This was the thing that led him to drive a bus, that impelled him to secure the 63 Venezia route, that sent him to that corner of the city, even on his days off. Once he had been bitten by the bug, he was a goner.

Argus had no experience with anything seriously like obsession or compulsion, and he felt its tight grip uncomfortable but irresistible. That distant vacant lot with its weeds and its cracked cement and its broken curbs and surrounding structures became the occupying thought of his mind, the center of his attention. Miss Meyers, Argus' teacher, noticed his distraction and tried to pry the secret out of him. Argus shook it off long enough to reassure her that he was merely reminiscing about a vacation and the wonderful time he had. She asked him to draw a picture of it, and the pile of crayons on his desk and the blank white paper before him became a great relief.

Argus drew cautiously. He was not the best at drawing. Molly was forever telling him that his efforts looked like nothing and she should just do exactly what she did. That little girl was never shy about offering her advice. Sometimes Argus would give in and copy her sketches of butterflies and horses and she would nod approvingly, and with her five-year old intensity assure him that he was making "great strides".

Argus liked to have friends, and he liked to tell his friends all his ideas. Max especially was continually astounded by the things Argus would say. Max believed that Argus was the smartest person who had ever lived, smarter even than Miss Meyers. When the teacher told him something new, he would double-check with Argus to verify the fact. Argus wanted so badly to tell Max about Snapdragon Alley. He didn't like this feeling all bottled up inside that he was not allowed to share or tell.

He drew a square in red, and then with brown and green he did some scribbling inside the square. With a yellow crayon he drew a tiny circle, and next to the circle, a stick figure of a man bent over, hand stretching toward the circle.

"What is that supposed to be?" Molly bugged him imperiously from his right.

"I like it", declared Max from the left.

"It's a place I know", said Argus, darkly hinting.

"Your room?" guessed Max.

"A sandbox?" Molly tried.

"It's a place my Uncle used to go and walk around", Argus told them. Suddenly he knew it wouldn't matter. Secrecy was an issue for the older kids, and certainly the parents had to be left out, but Max and Molly and Ayesha? It wouldn't do any harm to talk to them. Nobody ever believes us little kids anyway, he reasoned.

"What did you uncle do there?" Ayesha asked from across the table. She was always the one to catch on quickest when Argus had something of interest to tell.

"He was looking for something", Argus said, "something that no one else could see, and could only be found in a special way."

"Like hopping up and down on one foot twenty zillion times?" asked Max.

"Something like that", Argus smiled.

"Did he ever find it?" Ayesha asked.

"He did", Argus replied, "He found it but I think he lost it again, at least one time. He had to find it again and again. The thing kept getting away from him."

"Like my bunny rabbit", said Molly. "Every time I try to catch her, I almost get her and then she hops away. I have to grab her real tight but not too tight because I'm not supposed to squeeze."

"It hurts when someone squeezes you", Max supplied.

"Did you ever see it?" Ayesha wanted to know.

"Never", Argus said, and with that word he remembered Mason Henry, and what Sapphire said about the postcards, and thought that maybe he had said enough already.

"I don't really know what it was", said Argus, "that's why I can't really draw it. I can only draw somebody looking for it."

"It's a drawing AND a story", Molly declared approvingly. Argus could hardly believe she wasn't criticizing his work.

"Thanks", he said. He looked at the picture and decided it was finished. When Miss Meyers came over to ask him about the picture and what it represented from his vacation, Argus made up something about a playground and finding a toy in the grass, and he noticed that his friends were listening in and smiling quietly. They knew the difference between a story for your friends and a story for the grownups.

Sloppy Joes

Sapphire didn't feel the same way about it as Argus. She thought it was all very interesting, but also sad. Mason Henry was an old man who missed his wife and thought that maybe she was still alive and if only he could make the magic happen he would find her again and they'd be happily reunited. In short, she didn't really believe, and after all, she reasoned, why should she?

Obviously there WAS some kind of mystery involved. She had seen the name Snapdragon Alley with her own eyes on that one and only bus map, and Mason Henry's attitude towards selling the place fit in nicely with her father's story about the lot. She still liked her original idea that somebody had a proposal for a development and gave it that name. That person had some connection with whoever decides what goes on the map, and even if her father hadn't heard of it, that only meant the idea got lost in the bureaucratic shuffle somehow. She needed to get online and dive into the records. Even better, she needed to get into the office of urban planning and development and go through the files. Chances were the project had never been entered into any computer.

That was all going to be impossible, she decided, and so she filed the whole thing away in the back of her mind and concentrated on more immediate tasks - the volleyball team, swim practice, homework, and plotting more stray random notes to leave in stupid stores for unsuspecting customers to stumble upon. Those she composed during the classes she despised - Language Arts, for one. Math, for another. She tried to keep her snickering to herself, but on genuinely inspired occasions she couldn't help but kick the back of Alex's foot beneath the chair in front of her, and sneak him a copy of the note.

"Citizen Beware. These comestibles could be combustible!" - that one was for the shop that specialized in egg rolls and donuts.

"Any place has got to be better than this!" - that one was for World of

Flavors, a restaurant that only offered tomato soup, turkey legs, pancakes and ice cream.

She was going to wake somebody up. It didn't matter who. She was scheming to find a spy location where she could loiter and observe whoever was the first to discover the note, just to see the expression on their face. She could imagine it, and in fact her imagination was bound to be superior to reality (it always was), but just in case, in the off chance that for once reality might break through, she was calculating and planning.

Alex knew just what she was up to, and as they rushed to the cafeteria he almost blurted out "no way" even before she proposed the trip. Any spare time he had he wanted to devote to Snapdragon Alley.

"Oh, come on", she persisted. "It'll be fun. Besides, there's no way some invisible mystery land is suddenly going to pop up out of the blue and you know it."

"It's doesn't pop up", he replied, "it doesn't become visible to the whole world, only to the people who can see it."

"You mean to people who mutter some kind of mumbo-jumbo while pointing a coke can in the general direction of a dumpster?" she chuckled at her little joke.

"I know", Alex admitted. "It does seem stupid."

"Stupid, yes", Sapphire agreed and added with a terrible British accent, "but stupid in a rather sweet and delightful way"

This time she cackled so loud she almost choked.

"How come you never told me that your Uncle Charlie was such a weirdo", she asked after calming down.

"He wasn't", said Alex, annoyed. "He was a great guy. Everybody has their secrets, I guess".

"Not me", Sapphire said. "What you see is what you get", and with that she pushed her way to the front of the cafeteria line and was lost from Alex's sight. Just as well, he sighed. He had a feeling that they were not going to be seeing eye-to-eye on this one.

He didn't quite know what to make of it all himself. He knew it wasn't logical that a place like the one described by Mason Henry could exist in the way he said it did, and yet he knew from his own experience that there were lots of things that people couldn't see even though it was right in front of their faces. In Science class he learned that the human eye could only see a specific range in the spectrum of actual light, and that the human ear could only hear a specific range of sound. Dogs could hear sounds that people couldn't. Birds see things in ways that people don't. What if Snapdragon Alley was something like that - beyond the normal range?

In that case, why would it seem to be a housing development? Why would it appear differently to different people? What if it were an alien base that could project any kind of appearance it wanted to? That made some kind of sense, at least. It might have seemed to be a bunch of houses to Henrietta, when really it might have been a tangle of Martian seaweed or something. Maybe it was even a creature. Maybe it was a hungry beast that lured its prey right into its mouth. That could be what happened to Charlie, and Henrietta. Maybe it only got hungry once a year, and it was saving up for a tender meal of nice raw Mason Henry.

These ideas made the school lunch look even more disgusting than usual. The fact that it was sloppy joes and salad again didn't help. Alex couldn't even touch the stuff. He gnawed on a roll and chugged his milk while he sat off in a corner by himself. Sapphire had found the girls from her volleyball team and though she did smile and wave at him once, to let him know she was sorry about what she said about Charlie, and he sort of waved back to let her know it was okay, still he was glad to be all by himself for a change. He felt like he needed to sort through these ideas, to write them down and put them away. He pulled out his notebooks and made a numbered list of ideas. Later, in art class, he'd make up equations and formulas: if A then not B. If C and D then not A. Once he filled up pages with those, he'd be able to let the ideas alone to themselves, let them simmer and stew until one of them came bubbling up to inform him that it was the best of the lot.

Daniel Fulsom

All day, every day, whenever she ran into Alex, Sapphire had to listen to his host of theories about Snapdragon Alley and Uncle Charlie and the 63 Venezia bus line, so much she was getting sick and tired of the whole thing and really just wanted to prove to Alex, once and for all, that the whole thing was a big mistake, a complete misunderstanding. She was convinced that she could figure it all out, and to set the record straight, she took herself downtown to her father's office one afternoon after school. When she got there she forgot she should have told her father she was coming, because at first he wasn't there, and then when he was there he was busy with meetings and didn't have more than a second to talk to her.

This was really annoying because by that time she had already been waiting there for twenty minutes, sitting quietly in the visitor's chair near his secretary's desk, and Sapphire had worked herself into a state about that secretary, Crystal Wisburne, known to Sapphire secretly as Miss Whistlebottom. She was convinced that all too many of her father's late nights at the office were somehow the fault of this overly stuffed and overly perfumed sweetness. Sapphire had sat there scowling and trying not to breathe too deeply lest she get infected by the odor. And there were never any decent magazines at her father's office, mostly architectural and engineering rags. Who could get excited about steel frame buildings? Besides her dad, that is.

So after her father rushed through with nothing but a peck on the cheek and a homely 'sorry hon gotta run' little joke, followed by a closing of the door behind four identically balding men in suits, Sapphire was left half-standing half-stooping by the desk. Miss Whistlebottom gave her a friendly head toss which Sapphire scorned.

"Maybe I can help you with something, sweetie", mewed the cat-like secretary.

"Doubt it", Sapphire snapped, but Ms. Wisburne persisted and finally got it out of the girl that she was looking for the identity of the bus map artist, and really anything to do with a piece of land called Snapdragon Alley by some. As it turned out, to Sapphire's enormous surprise, Ms. Wisburne knew all about it.

The bus map artist was usually a boring firm called Hemp&Ether, but two years previous it had been farmed out for a special occasion to a fabulous specialist named Cyrilla Pak. It had been the fiftieth anniversary of Spring Hill Lake Transit Authority (SHLTA, pronounce Shlate-Ah) and the Authority wanted to celebrate with a dolled up bus map, among other niceties. Cyrilla Pak was famous, in her own right, having once done the transit map for the London Underground, not to mention the bus maps for Oslo, Stockholm and Brisbane, California. One could get in touch with Ms. Pak if one wanted, according to Miss Whistlebottom (and Sapphire was already beginning to feel guilty about that nickname), because Miss Whistlebottom (Wisburne, she told herself) had the artist's email address.

It may not be necessary, however, because, as Crystal Wisburne continued, she also knew about Snapdragon Alley.

By now, Sapphire was all ears.

"You've heard of it?" she was incredulous. "My father said there was no such thing! He says that plot was just a rundown apartment building that got torn down and now it's good for nothing".

"A decrepit tenement, yes", agreed Ms. Wisburne, "but most decrepit tenements don't just get torn down for nothing. There's got to be something in it for someone. Truth is, there was."

She leaned over her desk and lowered her voice to a whisper. Sapphire leaned over closer to hear.

"Your father won't remember, or at least he won't admit it. Wouldn't do him any good. Better not to know certain things. Better to forget. Especially when they involve a certain someone."

"A certain who?" inquired Sapphire.

"I really shouldn't say", Crystal Wisburne replied, "and I certainly wouldn't mention Mr. Daniel Fulsom's name to your father, if I were you." She winked, and Sapphire jumped up at the name. Of course she had heard of Daniel Fulsom. Everyone in Spring Hill Lake knew of the man who'd gone down in flames a few months before, along with the mayor and every single city councilman, who all turned out to have been on Fulsom's black market payroll. Unfortunately for him he had failed to buy off the chief of police or the chief's cousin, who happened to be the district attorney.

"I knew it!" Sapphire declared. "There WAS a project!"

"Oh most definitely", replied Ms. Wisburne, "no doubt about it. But then there was a tiny glitch in the plan."

"Mason Henry", Sapphire almost shouted, and even the all-knowing Crystal Wisburne was shocked.

"How do you know about him?"

"I met him", Sapphire said. "He said never. He'd never sell. At any price"

"Precisely", Crystal replied, nodding. "Curious that you met him, though."

"My friend has a thing about that place", Sapphire explained.

"Well, it might never come to anything", Crystal said, "with Fulsom in jail and Mason Henry hanging on to it. Sometimes a whole lot of nothing is all you get. Then again, it might be only a matter of time."

Now that she had her proof, Sapphire didn't need to hang around anymore, and she didn't want to have to explain herself any further to Miss Whistlebottom. She headed for the door and almost rushed off without even saying thank you, but Crystal had one more thing to tell her.

"You might want to get in touch with Cyrilla Pak anyway", she said, handing Sapphire a piece of paper with the artist's email address on it.

"She and your friend might have something in common", she hinted. "She had a feeling about that place as well."

Charlie Kirkham

Sapphire hurried home and stopped by Alex's house on the way to tell him what she'd found out, but he wasn't around. No one seemed to know where he was, but she guessed. He'd gone back to Snapdragon Alley.

Alex arrived there around three-thirty, after having to change buses twice due to breakdowns. He was feeling very subdued and calm, as if the unknown was just so enormous it was easier to let go and stop questioning. His mind had been racing for days around the idea of this place, and he'd resolved, this time, to keep his brain quiet and his eyes open and try to really see what was simply there in front of him.

And this time he saw the empty lot as merely an empty lot again. This time he noticed more clearly than before that the houses on Trent Boulevard were not just run down, they were almost all abandoned. Alex walked slowly past each one, walking up the steps and peering in the front windows, and taking note of the emptiness inside them all. Only the last house on the block seemed to still contain an occupant - Mason Henry's house. Alex knocked at the door and was not surprised that Mason Henry was not surprised to see him.

"Come in, Alex", the old man said. "There's someone here I think you'll want to see."

Alex followed him into the kitchen and then his predetermined calmness vanished in a heartbeat. Sitting on one of the folding chairs was his long lost uncle, Charlie Kirkham.

"Howdy, boy", Uncle Charlie said, slowly rising from his seat. He had barely made it to an upright position by the time Alex rushed over and flew into his arms. Alex could not hold back the tears and wept loudly into the grown man's chest. Charlie gave him a bug bear hug, but Alex didn't sense the old warmth he'd known so well, and soon let go, took a step back, and tried to get a clear look at the man.

Charlie was smiling, and Alex always remembered him with a smile, but was it the same smile? It had been two years, and two years are much longer for a child than for a grownup. Alex felt he couldn't trust his memories. Of course it was the same smile, the same man. If pressed, he would have had to admit that Uncle Charlie looked exactly the same as he had the last time Alex had seen him, down to the denim jacket, the two-day growth, and the yellowing teeth. He had a million questions and Charlie seemed to know it.

"Hold on there", he said, before Alex got a chance to ask them all at once.

"You might want to sit down, Alex", Mason Henry mentioned, and Alex did take a seat, as Charlie did, around the old aluminum table. Mason Henry puttered about as Charlie attempted to explain.

"Mason tells me it's been two years", he started. "That doesn't seem right to me. It seems like only yesterday I was sitting right here with him and Henrietta, talking about it."

"Everybody thinks you're dead", Alex blurted out, and Charlie stared at him.

"What do they think happened to me?" he asked, after a moment.

"They think you were offed by gamblers", Alex replied, and Charlie burst out laughing.

"Gamblers? What gamblers?"

"Because of your betting on the Sea Dragons", Alex explained. Charlie shook his head.

"That was just a pool among drivers and mechanics", he chuckled.

"Five, ten dollars here and there. Where'd they ever get such an idiotic notion? No, don't tell me", he held up a hand, "that darn brother of mine and his stupid wife - no offense, Alex. Forget I even said that." Charlie turned to Mason and said,

"My brother never could see past the end of a paycheck. If a man didn't make more money every year, according to my brother that man wasn't even fit to live. And the boy's mom", he continued, gesturing at Alex, "is just a walking disapproval machine as well. The two of them suit each other quite nicely", he smiled.

"But never mind that", he said, turning back to Alex. "Never mind all that. No, son, I am not dead yet, but I understand there's some confusion. Mason's been trying to explain to me about the time differential. Two years. I can hardly believe it. But now that I look at you, yes, I can see he's telling the truth. How old are you now, Alex?"

"Ten".

"You look more like twelve to me. I don't remember you looking so serious before. How's little Argus?"

"He looks more serious than me", Alex laughed, "and he's almost five now"

"Almost five, wow", Charlie whistled, "he's still a baby to me. Still in diapers. I can see it clearly as yesterday. In fact, I feel like I changed his diapers only yesterday. I was over at your house babysitting, wasn't I? We were watching a monster movie and you kept telling me how your mom and dad would be so mad if they came home early and caught us at it."

"Jompah the Wastelayer", Alex told him.

"That's the one. Jompah!" he laughed. "He was eating the villagers whole, I remember, and complaining about a lack of hot sauce."

"It was two years ago we watched that", Alex quietly said. "That was the last time we saw you."

"So it's true", Charlie nodded. "Thing is, Alex, like I was just telling Mason, it seems that in there," and he pointed towards the vacant lot across the street, "in there, there ain't no time at all"

Side View Mirror

Suddenly Charlie jumped up and rushed to the front of the house, where he just as suddenly stopped in front of the big picture window in the living room. Both of his hands were rapidly clenching and unclenching as he paced in place and said, to no one in particular,

"I've got to get back in there. I've got to get back."

Alex and Mason Henry followed him into the room and stood, side by side, staring at him. Alex was very confused. There was something definitely very changed in Uncle Charlie, who used to always be relaxed, easy-going, good-natured, or so Alex had always thought. This Charlie was intense, burning with a sense of urgency, and tumbling through his words rather than the old way he had of kind of gargling over them. It was difficult to explain.

"Did you figure it out?" Mason spoke up, and after a brief silence, Charlie turned around and faced them, shaking his head.

"First time that I went in", he said, "I thought I was just crossing the street. Boom, all of a sudden, there I was, somewhere else. Somewhere that hadn't even been there a moment before. Felt like I was only in it for a minute before it spit me out. Turned out I'd been gone a few days, missed a couple of shifts. Guys were wondering where I was. I couldn't really tell them anything."

"I thought it was the mirror", Charlie continued after a lengthy pause. "I mean the side view mirror in my car, because that was where I saw it first. Just a glimpse. I'd just parked my car and was heading over there to take a leak, tell you the truth. Just an old abandoned empty lot. No one around," he laughed.

"For some reason I glanced back at the car and there in the side view mirror was the place and not the lot. And when I turned back again, there it really was, all glass, plants and trees, and somehow I just walked right in. But the mirror thing never worked again after it pushed me out. I thought about maybe some other ways of seeing might do the trick. Colored glass. Prisms. Binoculars. Telescopes. Nothing worked. Time went by."

"And you met me and Henrietta out there", added Mason Henry.

"Yes, I did", Charlie agreed. "Henrietta thought she'd seen it too. Had a feeling, she did. So we got to talking about it. Between the two of us, we must have tried about every crazy thing just to try and catch a glimpse of something that nobody else would think was even real. It was real, all right. Still is."

"But what is it?" Alex blurted out. "What's in there? What are you talking about? I really don't understand."

Charlie looked over at him and smiled. Then he frowned. And smiled again. He didn't know how to begin, or whether he even should. Maybe he'd already said too much, he thought. This was not something for a child to know about.

"Alex", he began. "My boy. I don't know if we should even be telling you anything about this."

"But I already know something about it", Alex insisted, "You've got to tell me. I know it was on the map, and then it wasn't. I know that you saw something there, and you got stuck."

"Not stuck", Charlie interrupted, "not stuck at all. I'd give anything to get back."

"But why?" Alex repeated.

"What can I tell you?", Charlie said, "it won't make any sense."

"Just tell me anything", said Alex. "I'll believe you. I promise."

"It's everything", said Charlie, "in there, every thing is alive."

Alex was really lost now. Of course everything is alive. If it wasn't, it wouldn't be a thing. Or something. He had a feeling that Charlie was going to get even more confusing.

"Even the things you wouldn't think", Charlie continued, "like the bricks on the sidewalk. They make a pattern. They're sending signals. They have a meaning. The flowers, the pebbles, the walls on the sides of the buildings. The colors. You'd never know, but every little thing is really alive and communicating and feeling and knowing and full of purpose and direction. Everything fits together too. It's all one big living creature, all of this, the whole world, the universe, all of it. Nothing is outside, everything is within and connected. And moving. Everything is moving, in motion, all the pieces, all the particles, your skin, the air, the dust and shadows and specks of light. All of it is pieces, putting together, building, creating, making the world every moment, every minute, every day."

Alex was right. He had absolutely no idea what Charlie was talking about. Charlie might as well have been saying "phaw phaw phee phaw phoo". Everything is alive. Moving. Whatever.

Mason Henry was also lost, but he smiled and kept nodding his head as if he understood perfectly. Alex had the feeling that Mason would say anything to keep Charlie happy. After all, he was a lonely old man, and Charlie had been a good friend to Henrietta. He'd stayed by her side when she was sick, and never once complained or hesitated to do any favor that she might ask of him. Now that Charlie was back, Mason secretly hoped he would stay. He was in no hurry for Charlie for discover a way back in to Snapdragon Alley.

"But what am I saying?" Charlie asked himself out loud. He glanced over at Alex and chuckled.

"I had a feeling that would be a bit much for a kid. And anyway, aren't you supposed to be at home? How did you get here, anyway? It's a long way from your neighborhood."

"I took the 63 Venezia, of course", Alex said, and Charlie laughed.

"My old route", he said fondly. "Glad to know they haven't canceled it yet."

"It's usually pretty crowded", said Alex.

"Good, good", said Charlie, for no reason in particular. Just to say something normal for a change.

"We should be getting you home", he said. "It must be about dinner time already."

"I can get back by myself", Alex assured him, and Charlie seemed to be content with that. He didn't want to leave the area, not even for a second, just in case.

"Then you'd best be off", he told Alex, "and I'd rather you didn't tell anyone about all this."

"But my dad", Alex nearly shouted, "your own brother. He'd want to know you're still alive. They all think you died."

"I don't expect to be around very long", said Charlie. "Not if I'm lucky. Let 'em think what they already think. Won't do any good to tell them otherwise."

"Gee", said Alex. He wasn't sure he could keep such a gigantic secret. Charlie seemed to realized what he was asking, and added,

"Oh, don't worry. Go ahead and tell them if you want. I won't be angry if you do. If they want to see me. I'll be here, with Mason, at least for now."

"For as long as you want", said Mason.

"But when will I see you again?" asked Alex.

"I'll be right here", said Charlie, and then muttered to himself, "probably".

"Okay", said Alex, and he really didn't want to leave, and yet he really did too. Uncle Charlie was scaring him a little, the look in his eyes, and the weird things he was saying. Also, why did he want to keep his return a secret? Was there something else he wasn't telling him? Was he hiding from someone? Was he even telling the truth? Maybe he hadn't been in some mysterious place after all. Maybe he'd been in prison. Maybe he'd been in a loony bin. How could Alex know for sure? He really wanted to talk to someone else about it all. Really wanted to talk to Sapphire. She could help him sort it out.

And so he left. He got back on the 63 Venezia and made the connections back home and even made it there in time for dinner. His mom and dad had no idea he'd gone all the way across town after school. And he didn't tell them anything about Uncle Charlie either.

The 99 Forever

It was going to be a long evening, Alex thought, as he sat there silent across the table from Argus, while their mother and father had a long, intricate and deathly boring conversation about the real estate market in Spring Hill Lake in the recent decade. Argus had a way of picking at his food that usually caused his mother to scold him periodically, and the brothers played a timing game where they would try to guess when her next chastisement would arrive, flashing subtle hand signals as countdown mechanisms, but Alex kept forgetting to play and Argus finally just settled down and ate his food.

Later he tried to get his older brother to tell him what was on his mind because he could tell there was something, but Alex wasn't willing. He was even on the verge of snapping at Argus at one point, while pretending to be playing a game on the computer. He wasn't really playing, though, just watching the fish swim by without even killing or buying any, and he knew he couldn't blame Argus for trying. He just waved him off, saying "not now, okay?" and Argus let it go at that.

Alex felt like time weighed a thousand pounds and wouldn't get off his head. He carried that burden through a couple of pages of homework, and a half dozen pages of the book he was trying to read, and the light in the bedroom seemed incredibly bright and the quiet his brother was making seemed incredibly silent, and he felt like he was going to explode if he didn't do something quick. All he could think of was going outside for a walk, which is what he decided to do right when the telephone rang and he knew it was going to be Sapphire. He ran down the stairs, avoiding the call and rushed out the door right when his mother was yelling for him to get it.

Can't tell mom. Can't tell dad. Can't tell Argus. Can't tell Sapphire. But if I do tell, it would be okay. But I can't. Because I promised that I wouldn't. But he's alive!

The neighborhood was also too quiet and too dark, and there was nothing in it anyway. Just a typical urban residential sidewalk and single family dwellings of the kind whose value was apparently declining steadily. Maybe because they were boring. Maybe because they were ugly. Maybe because it sucked to live in this stupid little city with its stupid little shops and its typical array of parks and schools and offices and stoplights and cars and telephone wires and clouds and the sun that rises in the east every single stupid day.

He could only walk around the block two times before he was disgusted enough to go back home, where he snuck into the bedroom by climbing up the trellis and tapping on the window so that Argus would come and lift it. Argus did and after a glance realized that Alex was still in no condition to talk, so the little boy went back under the covers where he had a flashlight and a Spiderman cartoon book.

Alex just went up to the upper bunk and lay flat on his back, staring at the ceiling for the longest time, wishing that sleep could solve his problem but knowing that it couldn't. Tomorrow would present the exact same problem as today.

He finally did get to sleep, after what seemed like forever. And sleep was not a help at all. It gave him dreams, and in his dreams he sat there on a bus, and the bus was marked the 99 Forever, and there was only a handful of passengers scattered throughout the seats. The bus was making no stops, and outside the windows there was only blackness. Inside the only sound was the wheezing of the carriage and the rumbling of the wheels. Alex pressed his nose up to the glass so he wouldn't just see the reflection of his mournful face, but as he felt the cold glass touching him he also heard it, heard the glass say

"Hey, whatcha think you're doing? Get that smelly thing off me"

He pulled his face back and thought he could see another face in the window. Of course it was only his face, but it was talking. It was squinting at him, and he knew that the face only looked like his but wasn't him. The window face scared him, so he looked away, but now he saw his face looking right back at him from every little portion of the bus, from the seat covers, from the other windows, from the ceiling, from the advertisements pasted alongside the wall, from the handles on the doors, from the ridges on the rubber floor, all looking right in his direction, and suddenly talking, each of them all at once. The floors were complaining about people stepping on them. The railings were complaining about sweaty palms clutching them. The doors were whining about people pushing too hard against them, making it hard for them to stay closed, which after all was their job unless it was time to open, and then they would open, no need to shove. From beneath the floor he even felt the wheels grinding and their coating wearing away. He felt the bus itself growing old and being repaired, and oiled, and hammered at, and started and stopped and started and stopped until it was weak in the joints and its rivets were jostling loose.

Alex jumped out of his seat, just in time to hear it gripe about his jeans, which were scratching its nice shiny surface, and he ran up to the front of the bus, barely noticing that the other passengers sitting there calmly were nothing more than wax statues, mere images of people. He thought he would get some help from the driver but the driver was Uncle Charlie, and not Uncle Charlie but a kind of a painted wooden dummy version of Uncle Charlie which merely opened and closed its wide jaws, saying nothing but swiveling its head around like a ventriloquist's dummy.

"Everything is alive", the dummy head repeated. "Everything is alive".

Alex noticed that the bus was starting to go faster and faster, and that they were not on any street in any city, but nowhere whatsoever. Through the front window he saw nothing, not a street, not a building, not a light, not a road, not even a star in the sky. It was blankness and nothingness but even out there he sensed his own face, impossibly huge and looming, staring down at him, and telling him that if there were ever a good time to scream, that would be now.

The next thing he knew, Argus was beside him, shaking his shoulders as hard as he could, and Alex's eyes slowly opened and in the darkness of the night he was so happy to see his little brother's anxious face, he almost cried.

That was when he told Argus about seeing Uncle Charlie, and he told him everything that Charlie and Mason had said, and then he asked him what to do, the ten year old asking the five year old for advice. And in his calmest voice, Argus reassured his brother that everything was going to be okay.

The Witchcraft of Positive Thinking

Like every school day morning, Sapphire showed up before Alex and Argus were even out of bed. This tradition had been going on for years. It started as a favor to Sapphire's dad, that Alex's mom would walk the kids to school together in the morning so that Sapphire's dad could get to work on time, but by now it was more a force of habit than anything else. If it was a school day, she was there, entering the front door like it was her own home, bounding up the stairs and bursting into the boys' bedroom with a shout or a song or something new every day. This day was no exception.

"You are not going to believe this!" she yelled, and in two leaps was up on the top bunk shaking Alex and waving a piece of paper in his face. Before he even had a chance to say a word, she was off and running at the mouth.

"I found out about the artist of the artist map and I even got her email so I figured I would write her and get her story and oh my god you will not believe what she wrote back. I mean, almost immediately, before I even logged off last night. So I printed it out. Here. You have to read this!"

Alex was not quick enough for Sapphire. He had barely even opened his eyes and twitched a finger before she proclaimed,

"Okay, okay, I'll read it out loud, then. This is unbelievable. Hey, Argus, you too. Are you awake yet?"

"Mm hmm" the little one mumbled from the lower bunk. There was no way he could not be awake at the volume Sapphire was going.

"I mean, really", Sapphire said, "and when I talk louder it's because half the time she wrote in all caps, okay? I mean, when you hear me talking louder it's the caps. Now listen. No, wait. What I wrote was this. Dear Ms. Pak, because her name is Cyrilla Pak, so dear Ms. Pak, I have heard from a source that you were the artist responsible for the Spring Hill Lake public transit map of three years ago. In that map there was represented a street by the name of Snapdragon Alley which in fact does not exist. Can you please tell us the history of this addition to the map and its removal in subsequent years? And this is what she wrote:

"Child, for I assume you are a child, from what you have written and the tone therein - can you believe it? 'the tone therein'? - anyway, Child, I already said that, but, child, BEWARE (that's in caps). Take precautions that you do not meddle in secrets that are none of your affair. HE would not look kindly upon it"

"He?" Alex mumbled.

"Hold on", Sapphire said, "she gets to that. Where was I? Oh yeah, not look kindly upon it. It is a good thing you did not inquire about the magic, for then I would have had to tell you about The Witchcraft of Positive Thinking, and that would have led me to reveal even more terrible secrets that are not to be mentioned in public"

"I've heard of that", Alex said, "that's one of those self-help books. According to the author, in order to get what you really want, you have to be willing to pay the price."

"Funny", said Sapphire, that's exactly the words she uses here. HE is even now paying the price, and willingly, for the dream of HIS life to come true. HE gave me no choice, believe me, Child. For I have been illustrating bus maps for many, many years now, and never before have I entered upon such a dark and forbidding task as this one. To create the city. Ay. TO MAKE IT WHAT IT WILL BE, WHAT IT MUST BE, WHAT HE WILLS IT TO BECOME."

"All of that was in caps", Sapphire put in.

"I could tell", said Alex, now sitting straight up. "You were shouting".

"Oh, sorry", Sapphire said. "But anyway. It goes on. HE is in the dark dungeon now, but it is every bit a part of the plan. Did the factory close by itself? No. HE closed it. Did the homeowners abandon their homes? HE bought them out. All but one. And why? The answer lies in the DRAGONS"

"The dragons?" Argus was rubbing his eyes. "What dragons?"

"I think she means the football team", Sapphire said. "I've been putting some of the pieces together and, remember there was that vote about building a new stadium and everybody said no way, there's nowhere to put it?"

"Oh yeah, maybe", Alex shook his head.

"There's more than that", Sapphire said, "listen. Oh, HE knew what HE was doing when HE bought the rights, when HE paid the price, when HE bought them all."

"Do you see?" Sapphire asked, and Alex answered no.

"Daniel Fulsom", Sapphire continued, "the billionaire mobster. His plan is to build a giant shopping complex, AND a football stadium. Right there on Snapdragon Alley. That's going to be the name of the mall. Snapdragon Alley for the kiddies and moms, and Sea Dragons Stadium for the guys. It's all just a big redevelopment scheme, simple as that."

"But what about Mason Henry?", Alex asked.

"He's the last holdout", Sapphire said. "Without him, the plan can't go through, but he's old and he's got no heirs. Daniel Fulsom is going to get that land, sooner or later, one way or another."

"Oh no", said Alex. "But what'll happen to Charlie?"

"Charlie?" Sapphire was puzzled. "I thought ..."

"He's alive", Argus piped up from below.

"He came back", said Alex.

"And he's living with Mason Henry", added Argus.

"Then they're both in great danger", said Sapphire. "Listen to this. She goes on. HE is not patient. HE is almost done his time and when HE comes out, HE will strike, HE will act. HE has paid the price and now HE is going to get what is HIS. The Witchcraft of Positive Thinking will make it so."

"Beware, child. Forget about the map. Pretend you never saw it. Better yet, burn it. In two years time, then you will see it on the new map. Then it will be real, but far far better not to know, not to have known, not to have seen, not to have been. And whatever you do, Child, do not go to Snapdragon Alley. Do not go there. Do not go in. Stay away. Whatever you do. Stay away"

There was total silence for a few minutes after Sapphire read the last phrase and handed the paper to Alex, who looked it over for himself. There was no doubt in any of the children's minds. They were going back to Snapdragon Alley just as soon as they possibly could.

Mr. Quon

They had to wait until Sunday. For some reason, Alex and Argus' parents had decided that Saturday should be a "family activity" day. This was the first time all year and it drove the boys crazy. The last thing they wanted to do was visit the aquarium with mom and dad. The aquarium itself was fine - any opportunity to watch penguins was okay with them - but why now, why this day, and why with them? Mr. and Mrs. Kirkham clearly did not enjoy these little outings. Their dad spent most of the time muttering to himself and checking business e-mail on his cell phone, while their mom complained about the long lines at the ticket window, the long lines at the exhibit, the long lines to the restroom, the long lines at the cafeteria, and the horrible traffic back home. The day seemed endless, and by the time they did get home, it was only to find a voice message from Sapphire left every hour on the hour wondering where they were and when they could go "fishing", their pre-arranged code word for Snapdragon Alley.

Saturday finally petered out in front of the television with yet another nature special that their mother also thought would be "good for them", while she chatted on the phone with her friends and had a few of her special beverages. Alex and Argus waited until she'd gone to bed with a headache, and then they snuck into the kitchen to prepare a picnic for the Sunday adventure. They stayed up late, chatting about Uncle Charlie. Alex was worried about him, and Argus was merely anxious to see him.

Alex had good reason to be concerned. By the time the three kids arrived at Mason Henry's house the next morning, Charlie had been awake for more than seventy-two hours straight, according to the old man. Where previously he had paced throughout the house, now he stayed close to the front at all times, or stood outside on the steps, or ventured into the street, or wandered through the vacant lot itself. He carried a backpack filled with a variety of what he called "devices", but which looked like a random collection of ordinary things; a mirror, a magnifying glass, a telescope, binoculars, a blank book, a pencil, a compass, a flask, a fold-up umbrella, some toothpicks, a knife, assorted coins and paper clips, a toothbrush and a jar of Spanish olives.

Charlie certainly looked like someone who hadn't slept in days. His clothes were wrinkled and stinky. His hair was a mess, his beard unshaven. His eyes were bleary and he spoke in almost a whisper. Sapphire took one look at him as they bounded up the steps and said to Alex, in a low voice,

"He's gone nuts".

Alex did not reply. Argus was the first to reach the top of the stairs and ran into Charlie's legs, astonishing his uncle, who at first did not seem to notice the child at all. When he glanced down and saw the boy wrapped around his knees, he smiled and gave Argus a friendly pat on the head.

"My boy", he said, but looked back up immediately, scanning the horizon for any sign, anxious that he had missed something.

"Hi Charlie", Alex greeted him, and Charlie nodded in reply, but then suddenly took off down the steps and dashed across the street into the lot, leaving the children staring after him. Mason Henry appeared at the front door and offered to make them some hot chocolate. Sapphire accepted for the three of them, and after Mason had gone back inside she said to Alex,

"What do you think he's doing?"

"He's trying to get back in", Alex said. "It's all he wants to do. It's all he can think about anymore."

"Must be special", Argus murmured, but Sapphire snorted and said,

"Must be flipping insane". She had already made up her mind. The situation was pretty clear.

"The guy should be in a loony bin", she said. "Maybe he was. Maybe that's where he's really been the past two years. Not in some sort of time warp! A nut house!"

Alex had to agree it was a possibility. But he'd already checked. He'd called every asylum in the tri-state area asking that very question, but every one who would answer him said no, there was no record of a Charlie Kirkham, or even a John Doe meeting that physical description. He had checked the local hospitals too, and the prisons. There was simply no trace of Uncle Charlie in any of those places.

Mason Henry returned with a mug of hot chocolate for Argus, and Sapphire went into the house to fetch the others for Alex and herself. When she came back she found that a strange man had appeared at the bottom of the steps. He was a short, dark-haired man wearing a snappy suit and a seriously unfashionable fedora. He carried a slim black leather briefcase and did not smile at all at the children when he said,

"Is Mr. Henry at home?"

"Right here", Mason answered, gently pushing Alex aside and taking a place between the two older children.

"My name is Mr. Quon", the man announced. "I would like a word with you, sir".

He glanced menacingly at the kids before adding, "alone, if you please".

"We're not going anywhere", Sapphire replied, and put a hand on Mason Henry's arm, as if to protect him from some threatening harm.

"Very well, then", Quon continued. "I believe you know who I represent."

"I can guess", Mason Henry replied.

"My employer has allowed you one more opportunity for a reply in the affirmative".

"That's very generous", said Henry, "considering I own this property and there's not a damn thing he can do about it."

"I would not be so certain of that", warned Mr. Quon darkly. "My employer has many means at his disposal".

"I know about your employer", Sapphire burst in. "You tell him from me. We don't believe in his witchcraft. He'll never get Snapdragon Alley. Never!"

Mr. Quon cracked a smile for the first time, and addressed her directly.

"Well, young lady. Let me guess. You also have come to believe in this nonsense, this Loch Ness Monster of the Rubble."

"I don't know about that", Sapphire replied, "but you leave my friend alone. He's a good man who's never done anything to you or your employer."

"This is not personal", replied Quon, "but business. Mr. Henry is in the way of progress. We have offered, no, we continue to offer a most generous settlement. Every one else has already agreed. Look around you. All of the former residents of this block are now doing quite well in their new, upgraded homes. The factory over there, now happily relocated. This lot, this patch of dirt, will be the new home of the Sea Dragons, as well as a nice, friendly neighborhood of shops and new homes. There is nothing to fear. If you want to help the old man, convince him to accept. That would be best for everyone, believe me. We await your answer, sir".

And with that, Mr. Quon sharply turned and walked away, leaving Mason Henry looking weaker and older than ever. Sapphire helped him back into the house and sat him down in the easy chair to recover his breath.

"Why not settle?" she asked him, once he seemed himself again.

"Not yet", he replied. "Not until I know for sure."

"Know what?" she asked, but he only smiled in return.

"Bad news", said Alex, following them inside, with Argus remaining out front, eyes fixed on his uncle who was still wandering through the lot, periodically rummaging through his bag and holding up some object or other, before putting it back again.

"What?" Sapphire asked.

"That Mr. Quon guy", said Alex. "Before you came out he mentioned something about one week"

"One week what?" Sapphire asked. Alex shook his head, he didn't know, but Mason Henry did.

"One week until Daniel Fulsom's time is up", he said.

"You mean his prison term?" Sapphire asked.

"I'm afraid so", said Mason. "And he told me that I only had until then."

"And then what?" Sapphire wanted to know.

"They told me he had other ways of getting me out of the way, and they wouldn't hesitate to use them."

The Bus

Argus sat on the top step and watched Uncle Charlie perform his mysterious dance around the empty field. He understood it as a game of make-believe, except he knew that grownups never played that game, and didn't really know how. Charlie sure looked like he didn't. The whole point of pretending is that you know you're pretending so it's okay if it isn't real because you know it isn't, really, but Charlie didn't seem to be okay with it. He kept stopping in the middle of the game and cursing very loudly, words that Argus only otherwise heard from his father when he didn't get everything his way. Argus knew about not getting things his way. He'd been told that the youngest child gets spoiled, but not when the parents didn't really want that child, not when that child was just a nuisance and a burden and extra work. They had thought they were pretty much done with all that baby stuff when Argus came around. With him it seemed they just went through the motions, but Argus understood. He saw Alex and Sapphire going their own way and wanted to be just like them, to go with them, and here he was, again, snuck out of the house and all the way across town to see this wilder version of his father acting like a hungry chicken, strutting around, stopping and starting, occasionally crying out in his frustration and his despair.

Charlie did not believe enough. The other times he'd gone inside he'd just gotten lucky, or that's how it seemed to him now. He didn't know the rules, didn't know the game. He'd explained that all to Henrietta the last time he got booted out and had to hang around like this and try pretty much anything he could think of. Maybe the trying was all in vain. Maybe it would come when it would and there was nothing he could do about it. Maybe it just sucked him in and spit him out according to some crazy methodology he could never begin to guess at. In there, in there, what was it really all about in there? Was it what he thought? A piece of space and time ripped apart from the normal everyday, where the universal laws of nature were no longer universal, where the very facts of life were only half-assed guesses at some unfathomable mystery? Even in his time "in there" he'd gotten nowhere near the truth of it, could barely even remember now the beauty and the fascination and the spell of it. All he had to go on was the partial sense of having been in the only place where he should ever be, and of not being in there anymore. It's a kind of a post-partum depression, he thought.

Now he scoured the field for clues, for items, for anything that might turn out to be a link, unconscious of the staring eyes of the little child across the street, unaware of his long-lost brother, of his former life, of his old career, the Charlie Kirkham he had been and known. He was an other now. He was an other that shouldn't even be here, but should be there instead. Growing more dejected by the moment, and vaguely aware of the intense fatigue bearing down on him from failing to sleep or eat or even to lie down, he staggered back across the street to Mason Henry's house, where he rested for a moment on the bottom step. Argus quietly got up and came down to sit directly behind his uncle. For a few minutes neither of them moved or said a word. Charlie continued to gaze intently at the field across the street.

Quietly, Argus pulled an aluminum soda can pop top from his pocket, and held it out in front of his face. Through the hole he could see ... nothing, just what was there, but then he thought he saw something. At first it was like a pale green light, and in the pale green light he thought he could see a shape trying to form itself, a wavering in the air, a trend of empty air becoming solid mass. He held it out further away from his face and now it was in front of Charlie's too. Charlie made a motion to wave it away with his hand but he happened to glance at it, and through it, and he too saw the shimmering and he froze. He leaned his head back, so it nearly rested on Argus' shoulder. Cheek to cheek, almost, the little boy and his uncle watched through the pop-top as a very small and meager mist formed in the air above the vacant lot. The mist grew and seemed to hiss a little as it expanded, up and down, left and right, and became the size of a man, then the size of a van, then the size of a bus, the very size and shape of a bus only not just green but silver and green, like a city transit bus, and Charlie clambered to his feet, and as calmly as he could began to cross the street, but he was wobbling and trembling, terrified that the vision would vanish before he could get inside, because the bus was parked in the middle of the lot and it sure looked solid now and the driver's side door was facing him and open, and it looked like he could see somebody inside gesturing, waving him over. Charlie walked a little faster, and then even faster, and then he was across the street, and then in the lot, then almost at the bus and he didn't even notice that Argus was following right behind him.

Somehow, Sapphire just happened to look out the front window at that moment, and saw the man and the boy walking into the empty field and for some reason she could never describe later, she just knew it was wrong and she shouted out,

"Argus! Stop!"

But Argus didn't stop, and Sapphire yelled at Alex to "come on" and she raced out the front door and leaped down the steps and rushed across Trent Boulevard as fast as she could and grabbed the little boy around the waist, just as he was about to put his right foot down onto the bottom step of the bus.

"Let me go!!" Argus shouted and he struggled in her arms but Sapphire was too big and too strong, and then Alex caught up and grabbed Argus' legs to keep him from kicking Sapphire, and Argus kept yelling and screaming for them to stop and leave him alone and let him go, let him go, let him go, and then he was sobbing as he watched the bus door close, and the bus pull away, and he saw Uncle Charlie making his way to the back of the bus with the biggest smile on his face, and Uncle Charlie never looked back, not even once, and then the bus was gone. Vanished. Argus stopped fighting and sagged in Sapphire's arms.

"What was that all about?" Alex asked, and Sapphire shrugged, out of breath.

"I don't know", she said. "I don't know. But I just knew that we had to stop him"

"Stop him?" Alex repeated. "From what?"

"I don't know. I just couldn't take the chance", she said, loosening her grip, but still holding on to Argus arm as she led him back to Mason Henry's house. Argus followed listlessly but did not resist. He seemed completely drained. Alex kept trying to get Argus to tell him what was going on but Argus wouldn't answer. Even when they pulled him up the stairs and lugged him into the kitchen and sat him down in front of a glass of milk and a chocolate chip cookie, he just stared at the wall and wouldn't say a word. Sapphire and Alex looked on mystified.

Mason Henry came in from the living room and quietly sat down across the table from Argus. He stretched out his hand and patted Argus' hand softly.

"Charlie went back", he murmured, and Argus nodded.

Startled, Alex rushed back to the front of the house and for the first time noticed that his uncle was gone. He went back to the kitchen.

"Where?" he asked from down the hall. "Where did Uncle Charlie go?"

"Back inside", said Mason Henry. "Isn't that right, Argus?" he asked, and Argus nodded again.

"You saw him go in, son, didn't you?"

"It was a bus", Argus said and Mason Henry sighed. He looked up at Sapphire and Alex and said,

"I guess I'll never know now".

"Know what?" Sapphire asked.

"What happened to my wife", he said. "She went inside too. Went in with Charlie the last time. Charlie swore he doesn't remember that, but I saw her. Following behind him just like Argus was just now, and then poof, gone. Like that. When Charlie came back, I thought maybe Henrietta would too, but now I don't think so. Not with only a week left to go."

"What do you think will happen?" Alex asked.

"They'll tear everything down, rip everything up, pour in a lot of new concrete and put steel and glass on top of it all. We'll never see it again. It's all gone."

"It was a bus", Argus repeated, and for the first time he looked up at his brother.

"I didn't think it would be like that", he added.

"We couldn't let you go", Sapphire said. "I didn't see anything, but I knew."

"You did the right thing", Mason Henry told her.

"I wanted to go", Argus said, and he started to cry again. "More than anything", he blurted out. "I wanted to go".

Alex knelt down beside him and tried his best to comfort him, but Argus needed to cry, and he cried for maybe the first time since he was a little baby, and he cried enough to make up for all those years of never getting things his way.

Sea Dragons Stadium

It might have been the sorcery, or it might have been from paying off all the right people this time, but whatever it was, Daniel Fulsom saw his plans fulfilled. As he sat in the luxury box high above Sea Dragons Stadium ten years later, he proudly looked over the popular and highly profitable urban shopping mecca slash sports complex he'd built.

Snapdragon Alley, the name of the massive complex, was now on everybody's map, the talk of the town, the centerpiece of the city's economic revitalization, and his name, Daniel Fulsom, was in the headlines almost every day. He had become the legend he had always dreamed of becoming, and the price he'd paid was nothing to him now, a short time in prison, a temporary setback, some unpleasant but necessary dealings with a stubborn old man who now, god bless his soul, was resting in peace in some unmarked location unknown to his murderer's employer.

A young man also sat in the stands that day, along with his older brother and their friend. None of them were really football fans, but they put a few bucks on the spread in honor of their uncle's memory, and had a habit of visiting the streets around the stadium. The older brother was mostly interested in girls and beer these days, and drank a lot of the latter while he looked around at the former, while his friend occasionally jabbed him in the ribs when he was being especially obnoxious. The younger one stuck to soda, especially diet lemon lime, and liked to pop the tops off the soda cans and hold them up to the light, as if he expected to see something, as if the world could be different merely by looking at it in another way. After a moment he'd shrug, drop the tab on the concrete steps and say to himself, "well, you never know", and then pretend to be interested in the game again.